A. A. MILNE

Piglet Does a Very Grand Thing

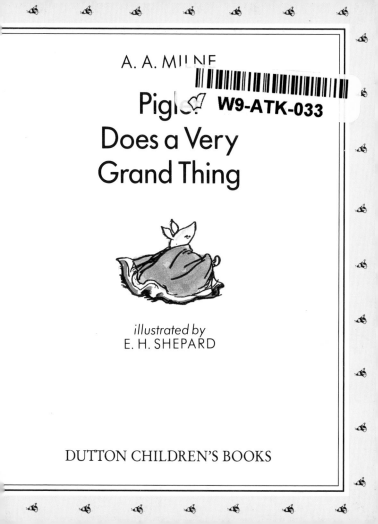

illustrated by
E. H. SHEPARD

DUTTON CHILDREN'S BOOKS

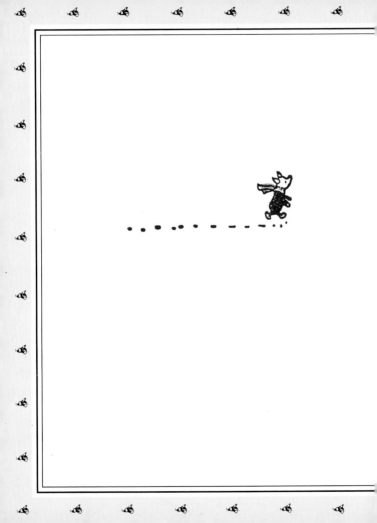

Piglet Does a Very Grand Thing

*Christopher Robin's friends in the
Forest included not only Pooh
and Piglet, but Eeyore the donkey,
(who was usually gloomy), Owl,
Rabbit (in whose house Pooh had
once got stuck because he was
so plump), Kanga the Kangaroo,
and Small, the Very Small Beetle,
(who had once been lost).*

Half-way between Pooh's house and Piglet's
house was a Thoughtful Spot where they met
sometimes when they had decided to go and see
each other, and as it was warm and out of the
wind they would sit down there for a little
and wonder what they would do now that they

had seen each other. One day when they had decided not to do anything, Pooh made up a verse about it, so that everybody should know what the place was for.

> This warm and sunny Spot
>   Belongs to Pooh.
> And here he wonders what
>   He's going to do.
> Oh, bother, I forgot—
>   It's Piglet's too.

Now one autumn morning when the wind had blown all the leaves off the trees in the night, and was trying to blow the branches off, Pooh and Piglet were sitting in the Thoughtful Spot and wondering.

'What *I* think,' said Pooh, 'is I think we'll go to Pooh Corner and see Eeyore, because perhaps his house has been blown down, and perhaps he'd like us to build it again.'

'What *I* think,' said Piglet, 'is I think we'll go and see Christopher Robin, only he won't be there, so we can't.'

'Let's go and see *everybody*,' said Pooh. 'Because when you've been walking in the wind for miles, and you suddenly go into somebody's house, and he says, "Hallo, Pooh, you're just in time for a little smackerel of something," and you are, then it's what I call a Friendly Day.'

Piglet thought that they ought to have a Reason for going to see everybody, like Looking for Small or Organizing an Expotition, if Pooh could think of something.

Pooh could.

'We'll go because it's Thursday,' he said, 'and we'll go to wish everybody a Very Happy Thursday. Come on, Piglet.'

They got up; and when Piglet had sat down again, because he didn't know the wind was so strong, and had been helped up by Pooh, they started off. They went to Pooh's house first, and luckily Pooh was at home just as they got there, so he asked them in, and they had some, and then they went on to Kanga's house, holding on to each other, and shouting, 'Isn't it?' and 'What?' and 'I can't hear.' By the time they got to Kanga's house they were so buffeted that they stayed to lunch. Just at first it seemed rather cold outside afterwards, so they pushed on to Rabbit's as quickly as they could.

'We've come to wish you a Very Happy Thursday,' said Pooh, when he had gone in and out once or twice just to make sure that he *could* get out again.

'Why, what's going to happen on Thursday?' asked Rabbit, and when Pooh had explained, and Rabbit, whose life was made up of Important Things, said, 'Oh, I thought you'd really come about something,' they sat down for a little . . . and by-and-by Pooh and Piglet went on again. The wind was behind them now, so they didn't have to shout.

'Rabbit's clever,' said Pooh thoughtfully.

'Yes,' said Piglet. 'Rabbit's clever.'

'And he has Brain.'

'Yes,' said Piglet, 'Rabbit has Brain.'

There was a long silence.

'I suppose,' said Pooh, 'that that's why he never understands anything.'

Christopher Robin was at home by this time, because it was the afternoon, and he was so glad to see them that they stayed there until very nearly tea-time, and then they had a Very Nearly tea, which is one you forget about afterwards, and hurried on to Pooh Corner, so as to see Eeyore before it was too late to have a Proper Tea with Owl.

'Hallo, Eeyore,' they called out cheerfully.

'Ah!' said Eeyore. 'Lost your way?'

'We just came to see you,' said Piglet. 'And to see how your house was. Look, Pooh, it's still standing!'

'I know,' said Eeyore. 'Very odd. Somebody ought to have come down and pushed it over.'

'We wondered whether the wind would blow it down,' said Pooh.

'Ah, that's why nobody's bothered, I suppose. I thought perhaps they'd forgotten.'

'Well, we're very glad to see you, Eeyore, and now we're going on to see Owl.'

'That's right. You'll like Owl. He flew past a day or two ago and noticed me. He didn't actually say anything, mind you, but he knew it was me. Very friendly of him, I thought. Encouraging.'

Pooh and Piglet shuffled about a little and said, 'Well, good-bye, Eeyore,' as lingeringly as they could, but they had a long way to go, and wanted to be getting on.

'Good-bye,' said Eeyore. 'Mind you don't get blown away, little Piglet. You'd be missed. People would say "Where's little Piglet been blown to?"—really wanting to know. Well, good-bye. And thank you for happening to pass me.'

'Good-bye,' said Pooh and Piglet for the last time, and they pushed on to Owl's house.

The wind was against them now, and Piglet's

ears

streamed

behind

him

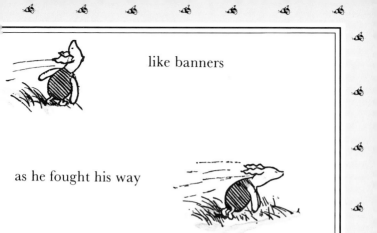

like banners

as he fought his way

along, and it seemed hours before he got
them into the shelter of the Hundred Acre
Wood and they stood up straight again, to
listen, a little nervously, to the roaring of
the gale among the tree-tops.

'Supposing a tree fell down, Pooh, when we
were underneath it?'

'Supposing it didn't,' said Pooh, after
careful thought.

Piglet was comforted by this, and in a
little while they were knocking and ringing
very cheerfully at Owl's door.

'Hallo, Owl,' said Pooh. 'I hope we're not too late for—I mean, how are you, Owl? Piglet and I just came to see how you were because it's Thursday.'

'Sit down, Pooh, sit down, Piglet,' said Owl kindly. 'Make yourselves comfortable.'

They thanked him, and made themselves as comfortable as they could.

'Because, you see, Owl,' said Pooh, 'we've been hurrying, so as to be in time for—so as to to see you before we went away again.'

Owl nodded solemnly.

'Correct me if I am wrong,' he said, 'but am I right in supposing that it is a very Blusterous day outside?'

'Very,' said Piglet, who was quietly thawing his ears, and wishing that he was safely back in his own house.

'I thought so,' said Owl. 'It was on just such a blusterous day as this that my Uncle Robert, a portrait of whom you see upon the wall on your right, Piglet, while returning in the late forenoon from a—What's that?'

There was a loud cracking noise.

'Look out!' cried Pooh. 'Mind the clock! Out of the way, Piglet! Piglet, I'm falling on you!'

'Help!' cried Piglet.

Pooh's side of the room was slowly tilting

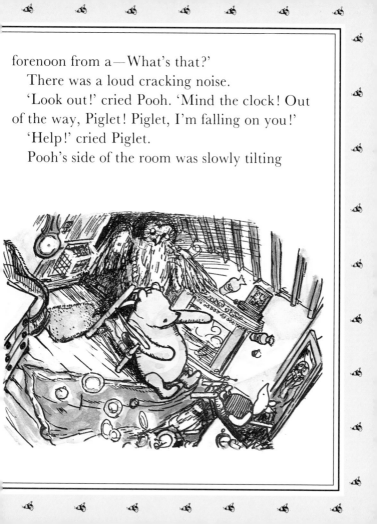

upwards and his chair began sliding down on Piglet's. The clock slithered gently along the mantelpiece, collecting vases on the way, until they all crashed together on to what had once been the floor, but was now trying to see what it looked like as a wall. Uncle Robert, who was going to be the new hearthrug, and was bringing the rest of his wall with him as carpet, met Piglet's chair just as Piglet was expecting to leave it, and for a little while it became very difficult to remember which was really the north. Then there was another loud crack . . . Owl's room collected itself feverishly . . . and there was silence.

In a corner of the room, the table-cloth began to

wriggle.

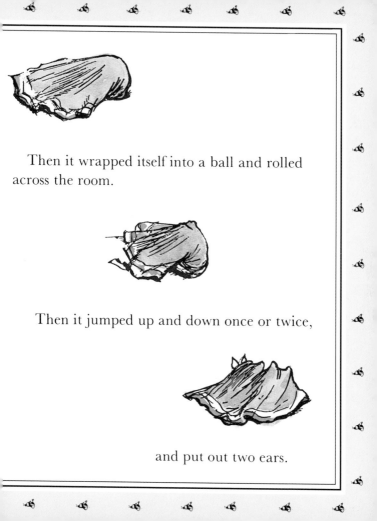

Then it wrapped itself into a ball and rolled across the room.

Then it jumped up and down once or twice,

and put out two ears.

It rolled across the room again, and unwound itself.

'Pooh,' said Piglet nervously.

'Yes,' said one of the chairs.

'Where are we?'

'I'm not quite sure,' said the chair.

'Are we—are we in Owl's House?'

'I think so, because we were just going to have tea, and we hadn't had it.'

'Oh!' said Piglet. 'Well, did Owl *always* have a letter-box in his ceiling?'

'Has he?'

'Yes, look.'

'I can't,' said Pooh. 'I'm face downwards under something, and that, Piglet, is a very bad position for looking at ceilings.'

'Well, he has, Pooh.'

'Perhaps he's changed it,' said Pooh. 'Just for a change.'

There was a disturbance behind the table in the other corner of the room, and Owl was with them again.

'Ah, Piglet,' said Owl, looking very much annoyed; 'where's Pooh?'

'I'm not quite sure,' said Pooh.

Owl turned at his voice, and frowned at as much of Pooh as he could see.

'Pooh,' said Owl severely, 'did *you* do that?'

'No,' said Pooh humbly. 'I don't *think* so.'

'Then who did?'

'I think it was the wind,' said Piglet. 'I think your house has blown down.'

'Oh, is that it? I thought it was Pooh.'

'No,' said Pooh.

'If it was the wind,' said Owl, considering

the matter, 'then it wasn't Pooh's fault. No blame can be attached to him.' With these kind words he flew up to look at his new ceiling.

'Piglet!' called Pooh in a loud whisper.

Piglet leant down to him.

'Yes, Pooh?'

'*What* did he say was attached to me?'

'He said he didn't blame you.'

'Oh! I thought he meant—Oh, I see.'

'Owl,' said Piglet, 'come down and help Pooh.'

Owl, who was admiring his letter-box, flew down again. Together they pushed and pulled at the armchair, and in a little while Pooh came out from underneath, and was able to look round him again.

'Well!' said Owl. This is a nice state of things!'

'What are we going to do, Pooh? Can you think of anything?' asked Piglet.

'Well, I *had* just thought of something,' said Pooh. 'It was just a little thing I thought of.' And he began to sing:

I lay on my chest
And I thought it best
To pretend I was having an evening rest;
I lay on my tum
And I tried to hum

But nothing particular seemed to come.
My face was flat
On the floor, and that
Is all very well for an acrobat;
But it doesn't seem fair
To a Friendly Bear
To stiffen him out with a basket-chair.
And a sort of sqoze
Which grows and grows
Is not too nice for his poor old nose,
And a sort of squch
Is much too much
For his neck and his mouth and his ears and such.

'That was all,' said Pooh.

Owl coughed in an unadmiring sort of way, and said that, if Pooh was sure that *was* all, they could now give their minds to the Problem of Escape.

'Because,' said Owl, 'we can't go out by what used to be the front door. Something's fallen on it.'

'But how else *can* you go out?' asked Piglet
anxiously.

'That is the Problem, Piglet, to which I

am asking Pooh to give his mind.'

Pooh sat on the floor which had once been a
wall, and gazed up at the ceiling which had
once been another wall, with a front door in it
which had once been a front door, and tried to
give his mind to it.

'Could you fly up to the letter-box with
Piglet on your back?' he asked.

'No,' said Piglet quickly. 'He couldn't.'

Owl explained about the Necessary Dorsal
Muscles. He had explained this to Pooh and

Christopher Robin once before, and had been
waiting ever since for a chance to do it again,
because it is a thing which you can easily
explain twice before anybody knows what you
are talking about.

'Because you see, Owl, if we could get Piglet
into the letter-box, he might squeeze through
the place where the letters come, and climb
down the tree and run for help.'

Piglet said hurriedly that he had been getting
bigger lately, and couldn't *possibly*, much
as he would like to, and Owl said that he

had had his letter-box made bigger lately in case he got bigger letters, so perhaps Piglet *might*, and Piglet said, 'But you said the necessary you-know-whats *wouldn't*,' and Owl said, 'No, they *won't*, so it's no good thinking about it,' and Piglet said, 'Then we'd better think of something else,' and began to at once.

But Pooh's mind had gone back to the day when he had saved Piglet from the flood, and everybody had admired him so much; and as that didn't often happen, he thought he would like it to happen again. And suddenly, just as it had come before, an idea came to him.

'Owl,' said Pooh, 'I have thought of something.'

'Astute and Helpful Bear,' said Owl.

Pooh looked proud at being called a stout and helpful bear, and said modestly that he just happened to think of it. You tied a piece of string to Piglet, and you flew up to the letter-box, with the other end in your beak, and you pushed it through the wire and brought it down to the floor, and you and Pooh pulled hard at this end, and Piglet went slowly up at the other end. And there you were.

'And there Piglet is,' said Owl. 'If the string doesn't break.'

'Supposing it does?' asked Piglet, really wanting to know.

'Then we try another piece of string.'

This was not very comforting to Piglet, because however many pieces of string they tried pulling up with, it would always be the same him coming down; but still, it did seem the only thing to do. So with one last look back in his mind at all the happy hours he had spent in the Forest *not* being pulled up to the ceiling by a piece of string, Piglet nodded bravely at Pooh and said that it was a Very Clever pup-pup-pup Clever pup-pup Plan.

'It won't break,' whispered Pooh comfortingly, 'because you're a Small Animal, and I'll stand underneath, and if you save us all, it will be a Very Grand Thing to talk about afterwards, and perhaps I'll make up a Song, and people will say "It was so grand what Piglet did that a Respectful Pooh Song was made about it!"'

Piglet felt much better after this, and when everything was ready, and he found himself slowly going up to the ceiling, he was *so* proud

that he would have called out 'Look at *me*!' if he hadn't been afraid that Pooh and Owl would let go of their end of the string and look at him.

'Up we go!' said Pooh cheerfully.

'The ascent is proceeding as expected,'
said Owl helpfully.

Soon it was over. Piglet opened the letter-
box and climbed in. Then, having untied

himself, he began to squeeze into the slit,
through which in the old days when front
doors *were* front doors, many an unexpected
letter that WOL had written to himself, had
come slipping.

He squeezed and he sqoze, and then with one

last squze he was out.
Happy and excited he
turned round to squeak
a last message to
the prisoners.

'It's all right,' he called through the
letter-box. 'Your tree is blown right over,
Owl, and there's a branch across the door, but

Christopher Robin and I can move it, and we'll
bring a rope for Pooh, and I'll go and tell him
now, and I can climb down quite easily, I
mean it's dangerous but I can do it all right,

and Christopher Robin and I will be back in about half an hour. Good-bye, Pooh!' And without waiting to hear Pooh's answering 'Good-bye, and thank you, Piglet,' he was off.

'Half an hour,' said Owl, settling himself comfortably. 'That will just give me time to finish that story I was telling you about my Uncle Robert—a portrait of whom you see underneath you. Now let me see, where was I? Oh, yes. It was on just such a blusterous day as this that my Uncle Robert—'

Pooh closed his eyes.